JUDY and the VOLCANO

Wayne Harris

SCHOLASTIC
SYDNEY AUCKLAND NEW YORK TORONTO LONDON

For Pete Nettell

Harris, Wayne.
    Judy and the volcano.

    ISBN 1 86388 310 X.
    ISBN 1 86388 311 8 (pbk.).

    I. Title.

A823.3

First published in 1994 by Scholastic Australia Pty Limited ACN 000 614 577,
PO Box 579, Gosford 2250. Also in Sydney, Brisbane, Melbourne, Adelaide
and Perth.

Reprinted in 1995 and 1996.

Packaged for Scholastic Australia by Donna Rawlins.

This book was typeset in Uniform C57.

The illustrations for this book were painted with acrylics.

Typeset by Asset Typesetting Pty Ltd, Sydney.

Printed in Singapore.

9 8 7 6 5 4 3   6 7 8 9 / 9

When it comes to writing stories there is no doubt about who is going to get top marks. It's Madeleine Corsy. ALWAYS Madeleine Corsy.

I can't **stand it!**

Mrs Be-the-best-you-can
always says,
'Madeleine's got imagination'.
Well so what? I've got it too.
Once I wrote my whole
story in invisible ink.

All Madeleine's got
is fairies and elves
on the brain.
Well I've never seen a fairy
yet. I wish I *could*.
But she's so smart;
like that story she wrote
where she was fed honey
on spoons by nine fairies in
dresses made of cobwebs.

What *I* wanted to know was
where was the spider
while all this was going on?

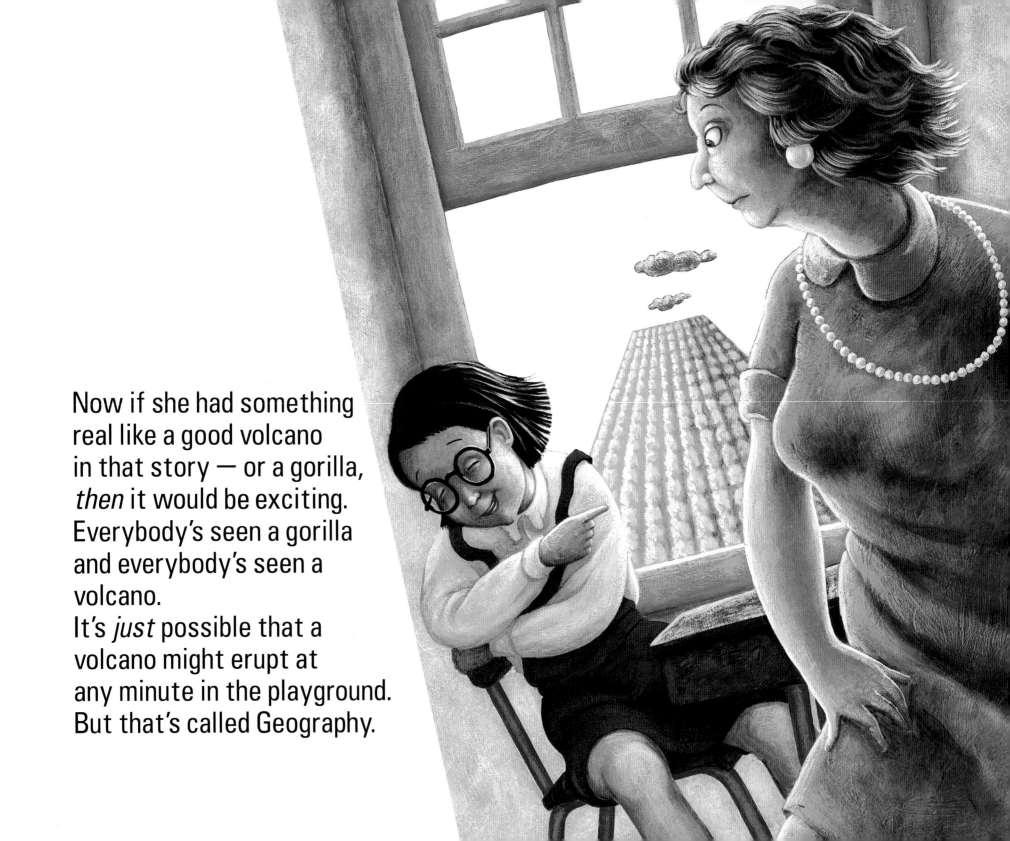

Now if she had something
real like a good volcano
in that story — or a gorilla,
then it would be exciting.
Everybody's seen a gorilla
and everybody's seen a
volcano.
It's *just* possible that a
volcano might erupt at
any minute in the playground.
But that's called Geography.

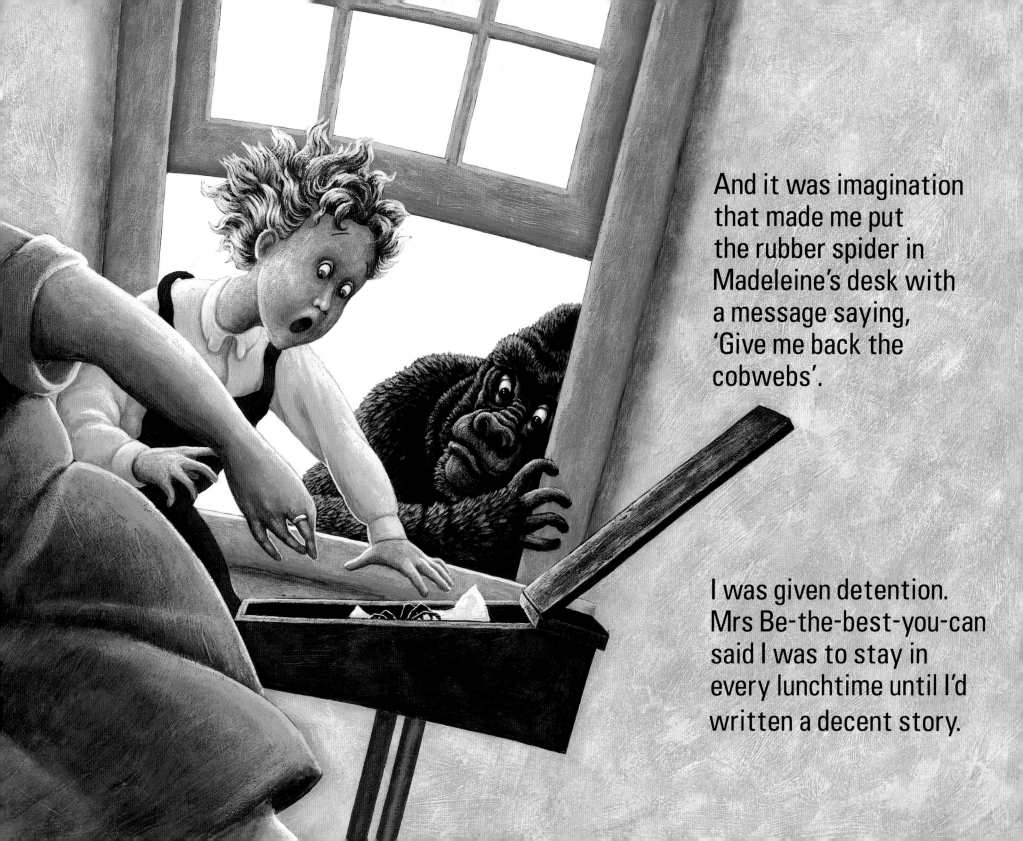

And it was imagination that made me put the rubber spider in Madeleine's desk with a message saying, 'Give me back the cobwebs'.

I was given detention. Mrs Be-the-best-you-can said I was to stay in every lunchtime until I'd written a decent story.

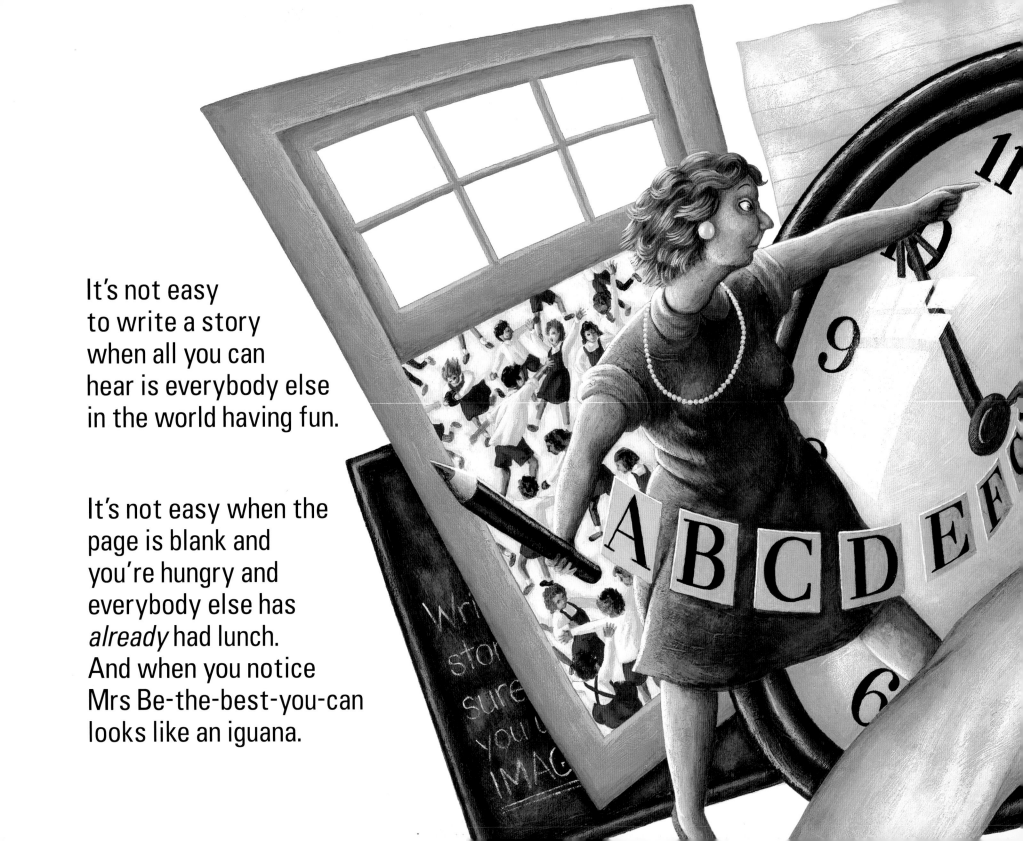

It's not easy
to write a story
when all you can
hear is everybody else
in the world having fun.

It's not easy when the
page is blank and
you're hungry and
everybody else has
already had lunch.
And when you notice
Mrs Be-the-best-you-can
looks like an iguana.

The next day I wrote
that giant tree vines
had grown around my legs
and arms and the
volcano was spurting
red-hot lava around the
island and all the
children were yelling out,

'Save us Judy Marx!'

I had a good mind to
stay just where I was.

After lunch Madeleine Corsy
said to me,
'I hope your story is good
Judy Marx, so you can
come and play tomorrow,'
and I said,
'The story's terrific!'

But somehow I knew
she thought I was just being
imaginative.

But I couldn't think what to write next. I wanted to put a **gorilla** into the story, and maybe a **volcano,** but it was too hard to think how.

'...and I'm the only one
who can rescue all the
children from the giant
iguana.'
But I didn't say that
all the children looked
like Madeleine Corsy
and that the iguana
looked like
you know who.
This was
getting to be fun.

Then I put, 'I'm caught in the...
worst storm the world has ever seen!'

On the second lunchtime
when everyone else was playing
adventure games I wrote,
'My name's Judy Marx and I'm...'

I couldn't think of anything
to write after that.

And that awful clock
says you've only ten
minutes left and you
can't think of anything
to write.
I tell you it's not easy.

And then Madeleine
comes up to you and
smiles and says,
'I forgive you Judy Marx'.

Well really, if it wasn't
for Madeleine Corsy being
so good I wouldn't be in
this mess.

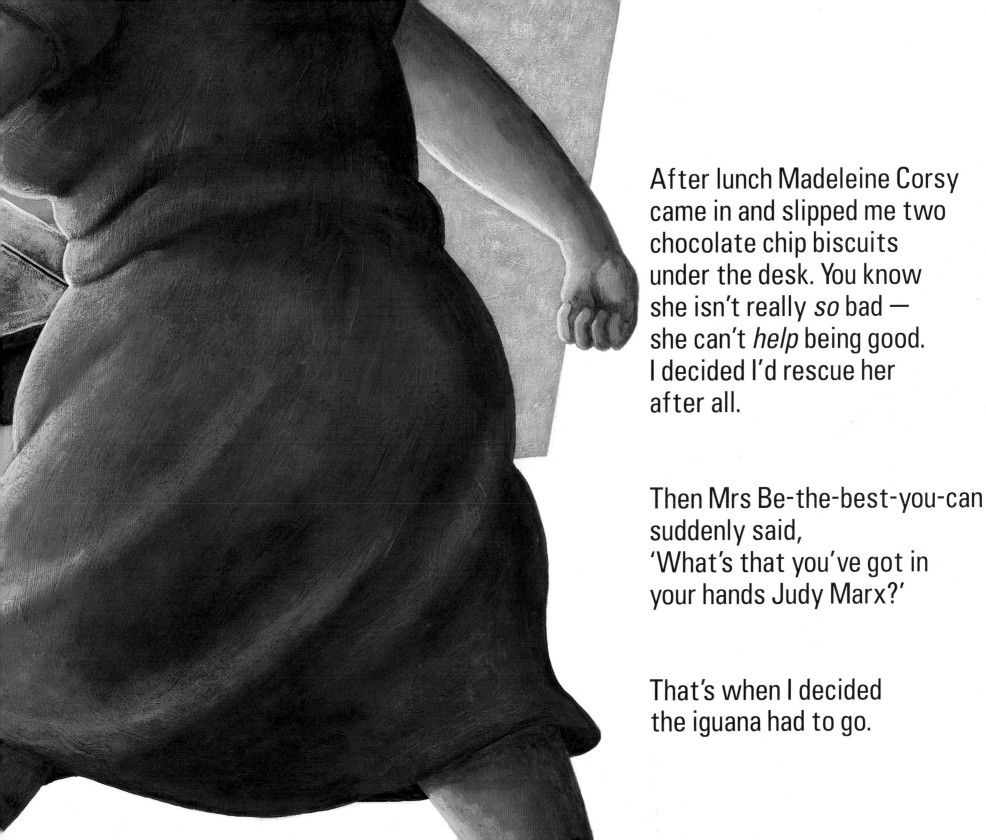

After lunch Madeleine Corsy
came in and slipped me two
chocolate chip biscuits
under the desk. You know
she isn't really *so* bad —
she can't *help* being good.
I decided I'd rescue her
after all.

Then Mrs Be-the-best-you-can
suddenly said,
'What's that you've got in
your hands Judy Marx?'

That's when I decided
the iguana had to go.

I imagined rain pouring
down on the hot lava and
turning into great clouds
of hissing steam. I made
one gigantic effort to
break the vines with my
enormous strength.
Then the iguana appeared
and...

lunchtime was over,
and everybody came in to
class looking very happy
with themselves.
That was okay because
I was beginning to feel very
happy with myself too.

Madeleine asked me how
my story was going and I
told her that
Mrs Be-the-best-you-can
was an iguana and I was
about to trap her.
We both giggled but then
Mrs Be-the-best-you-can
trapped both *of us* and said,
'You two girls come out
the front!'
Caught again.

She said,
'Tomorrow I want you and
Madeleine to read your stories
to the school assembly'.
And then she smiled.

Odd.
When Mrs Be-the-best-you-can
smiles she doesn't look like
an iguana at all.
The iguana just disappears.

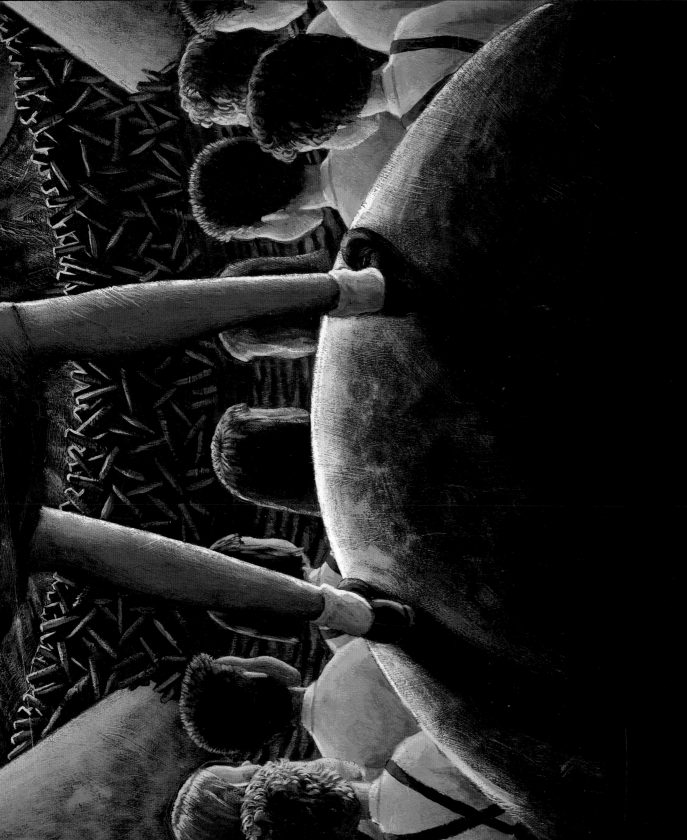

So that afternoon I wrote that I dammed up all the rivers on the island and stopped the lava from causing any harm. The children were safe and the iguana was free to roam on its own land.

After all iguanas aren't so bad.

The two gold stars
for Madeleine and me
were nearly as exciting
as everyone clapping.

I couldn't wait to get
started on my new story...

It's about a **gorilla** who rescues two **famous writers** from a... **giant cobweb.**